Tim Rows a Boat Gently Down the Stream

Characters

Narrator

Tim

Friend 1

Friend 2

Friend 3

Dad

Setting

Tim's bedroom; a stream (in a dream)

Picture Words

boat

row

Sight Words

| can | come | I | in |
| like | see | today | want |

shore

stream

Enrichment Words

dream

gently

merrily

wake up

Narrator: Then Tim's dad called out to him.

Dad: Tim! Tim! Come home.

Friend 1: We want to row and row.

Friend 2: I like to row my boat.

Friend 3: Row, row, row.

Narrator: In Tim's dream, Tim and his friends rowed merrily back to the shore.

Tim: Look! I see a butterfly.

Friend 1: I see a rabbit.

Friend 2: I see a snail.

Friend 3: Can I see?

Narrator: Suddenly Tim opened his eyes. His dad was in his bedroom.

Dad: Tim! Wake up. Today is a big day.

Tim: Yes!

Dad: Today we will row a boat.

The End